THE 12 BIGGEST BREAKTHROUGHS IN
GAMING TECHNOLOGY

by Jamie Kallio

12 STORY LIBRARY

www.12StoryLibrary.com

12-Story Library is an imprint of Bookstaves.

Photographs ©: logoboom/Shutterstock.com, cover, 1; Edward Blake/CC2.0, 4; CM/Associated Press, 5; Eric Risberg/Associated Press, 6; Yuri_Arcurs/iStockphoto, 7; CTR Photos/Shutterstock.com, 8; CTRPhotos/iStockphoto, 9; AnthonyRosenberg/iStockphoto, 10; Mika1h/CC3.0, 11; ArcadeImages/Alamy Stock Photo, 12; Atari, Inc., 12; OlegDoroshin/Shutterstock.com, 13; picturesbyrob/Alamy Stock Photo, 14; BagoGames/CC2.0, 15; Jamaway/Alamy Stock Photo, 16; Iryna Tiumentseva/Shutterstock.com, 17; Zhenikeyev/iStockphoto, 18; Spencer_Whalen/iStockphoto, 19; LightFieldStudios/iStockphoto, 20; PD, 21; Wachiwit/iStockphoto, 22; dennizn/Shutterstock.com, 23; RyanKing999/iStockphoto, 24; MSSA/Shutterstock.com, 24; Mano Kors/Shutterstock.com, 25; Gorodenkoff/Shutterstock.com, 26; marcello farina/Shutterstock.com, 27; Tinxi/Shutterstock.com, 28; scyther5/iStockphoto, 29

ISBN
978-1-63235-582-9 (hardcover)
978-1-63235-636-9 (paperback)
978-1-63235-696-3 (hosted ebook)

Library of Congress Control Number: 2018937980

Printed in the United States of America
Mankato, MN
June 2018

Access free, up-to-date content on this topic plus a full digital version of this book. Scan the QR code on page 31 or use your school's login at 12StoryLibrary.com.

Table of Contents

Game Consoles Bring Video Games Home

Before there was home gaming, people played video games at arcades. In 1972, a company called Magnavox released the first home game console. This was a small computer system that connected to a television. The console was called the Magnavox Odyssey. Games were made up of just dots and lines.

One of the most popular arcade games was Atari's *Pong*. In 1975, Atari sold a home version of the game. *Pong* was similar to tennis. Players used paddles to hit a ball over a net. The game had two-dimensional (2D) graphics. In 1977, Atari released a console that played other games. *Space Invaders* and *Missile Command* became popular.

In 1985, a Japanese company released a new home gaming console. The console's name was

EXPERIENCE FOR ALL AGES

A Magnavox Odyssey.

THE BROWN BOX

The Magnavox Odyssey had a life before 1972. Engineer Ralph Baer had created the console in 1967. It was originally called the Brown Box. The Brown Box had simple games. In one game, two squares chased each other across the screen. Baer later allowed Magnavox to release the console.

the Nintendo Entertainment System. It became the best-selling console in history. Nintendo released many popular games. These included *Super Mario Bros.* and *The Legend of Zelda*.

Nintendo followed its home game console with other devices. One of them, called the Game Boy, was handheld. Other companies released consoles, too. These companies included Sega Genesis, PlayStation, and Xbox. New technology gave each console better sound and graphics.

150,000
Number of Atari consoles sold during the 1975 holiday season.

- Magnavox Odyssey was the first home game console.
- Atari's *Pong* was a popular game in the 1970s.
- The first Nintendo console came out in 1985.
- The PlayStation and Xbox consoles came out after Nintendo.

PC Gaming Becomes Popular

Home video games can be played on a console or on a personal computer (PC). In the 1980s, PC gaming became popular. Affordable computers, such as the Apple II, were released. These home computers had powerful processors. Video games became more complex. As early as 1987, PC gamers could play multiplayer online games.

PC games are usually cheaper than console games. There is a wider variety of PC games to choose from. Some gamers prefer a keyboard and mouse to a console game controller. They think the PC devices have better accuracy. Graphics are also sharper on a computer.

THINK ABOUT IT

Do you prefer a PC or a game console? Use information from this chapter to compare and contrast the two types. Is there a specific brand you would choose over others?

Building a gaming PC can be expensive. PCs need updated operating systems for gaming.

Game consoles are much cheaper. Most game consoles today sell for under $500. A good gaming PC can cost twice as much. Game consoles are also easier to set up. Gamers can begin play almost immediately. Both PCs and game consoles have their advantages. Some players may prefer one or the other. Others enjoy using both.

$30,000
Cost of the 8Pack OrionX, the most expensive gaming PC ever built.

- Many people prefer to play video games on a PC.
- PC games are cheaper to purchase than console games.
- A wide variety of PC games are available.
- Building a good gaming PC can be expensive.

Cartridges Give Way to DVDs

When home gaming consoles first came out, games came on cartridges. Cartridges are plastic, box-like devices that plug into a console. In 1976, Fairchild Electronics created the first video game cartridges. Gamers could now use multiple games in the same console. Handheld devices also used cartridges.

Cartridges went through many changes. Some cartridges were very large. Others were small. No matter their size, cartridges were durable. They also loaded games quickly. However, cartridges had some problems. They became dirty with use. Their springs would wear out. This weakened the connection between the cartridge and the console. Sometimes the game would not work.

In the early 1990s, Sega and Sony created units that used CD-ROMs. In 2000, Sony released the PlayStation 2 (PS2). The PS2 used DVDs instead of CD-ROMs. This meant gamers

could play games and watch DVDs on the same unit. The PS2 became extremely popular. It replaced many families' DVD players.

Nintendo stopped releasing game cartridges in 1996. The company switched to CD-ROMs and DVDs instead. However, cartridges made a comeback. In 2017, the Nintendo Switch console came out. This console used cartridges.

157 million
Number of PlayStation 2s sold as of 2017.

- Before DVDs, games came on cartridges.
- Game cartridges were durable and delivered information quickly.
- Cartridges could wear out.
- CD-ROMs and DVDs replaced cartridges.

Controllers Take Many Forms

Game controllers allow players to control characters on the screen. All video games require a controller. Types of controllers vary widely. Early controllers had to be attached to the game console by a cord. In the late 1970s, Atari released the first wireless controller.

The joystick was a popular game controller in the 1970s. It had a heavy square base with a stick in the center. The stick pointed upward and moved in eight directions. Joysticks could be uncomfortable. They often put strain on the player's wrist.

In 1985, Nintendo introduced the first gamepad. A gamepad is a controller with multiple buttons. Most modern gamepads include

Joysticks often put strain on a player's wrist.

a D-pad. This is a cross-shaped set of four buttons. It allows players to move left, right, up, and down. In 1997, Nintendo released the Rumble Pak. This gamepad vibrated during certain parts of games.

Controllers for rhythm games have special features. *Dance Dance Revolution* requires players to step on a dance pad. *Guitar Hero* uses a plastic controller shaped like a guitar. The controller makes players feel like they are creating music.

1997

Year that the first rhythm game, *PaRappa the Rapper*, was released.

- All video games require a game controller.
- The joystick and the D-pad were some of the first game controllers.
- Rhythm game controllers are very different from standard controllers.

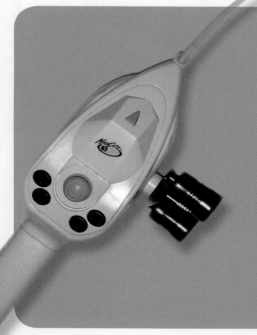

ODD CONTROLLERS

The controller for Sega's game *Bass Fishing* looked like a fishing rod. It could recognize players' motions. Nintendo's Power Glove also recognized motion. Players wore a glove that was connected to a controller. The glove allowed players to control the game with hand motions. Neither the Power Glove nor the fishing rod worked very well. Both controllers were discontinued.

Graphics Become More Realistic

Computer graphics use data to create images on a screen. In early games, simple shapes floated on a black screen. In 1977, *Super Bug* by Kee Games became the first game to feature scrolling. In *Super Bug*, the player drove a car while the background scrolled behind it.

As technology advanced, so did graphics. Bitmaps improved over the years. Bitmaps are digital images made up of a grid of dots. Higher-resolution bitmaps gave objects more depth. In 1987, the computer company IBM created Video Graphics Array (VGA). VGA was a display system that could show 256 colors at once. This was a big improvement. Older systems showed

Super Bug was the first video game to use a scrolling playfield.

THINK ABOUT IT

Use the internet to learn more about CGI. How has it been used in movies and television? How is CGI in movies different from or similar to CGI in video games?

only 16 colors. Increased computer memory also improved graphics.

Over the years, video game graphics have become more realistic. Today most games use computer-generated imagery (CGI). CGI creates the appearance of a three-dimensional (3D) world. It uses effects such as lighting, shadows, and reflection. The results are similar to graphics in many movies.

1972

Year that animation studio Pixar created the first 3D image of a hand.

- Computer graphics use data to display images on a digital screen.
- Early video game graphics were very simple.
- New technology allowed for better graphics.
- Video games use CGI to create 3D environments.

13

Motion Control Lets Players In on the Action

In motion control games, players use body movements to control characters' actions. Motion control allows players to physically experience video games. In 2006, Nintendo released a motion control console called the Wii. *Wii Sports* became one of the most popular games in history.

Wii Sports includes tennis, baseball, bowling, golf, and boxing. Players hold a remote that detects

82.8 million

Number of *Wii Sports* sold worldwide as of 2017.

- Motion control video games allow players to physically experience the game.
- Nintendo's *Wii Sports* became one of the most popular games in history.
- Some critics think motion control games are too simple.
- Many new VR games require the use of motion controls.

THINK ABOUT IT

Define the term "casual gamers." What does it mean? Why do you think casual gamers are drawn to motion control games?

movements, such as waving and tilting. The movements are communicated to the game through a wireless connection. In *Wii Tennis*, the player swings the remote like a racket. The avatar on the screen makes the same motion. Other motion control devices are Sony's PlayStation Move and Microsoft's Kinect for Xbox 360 and Xbox One.

Motion control games drew a large crowd of casual gamers. The games' focus on natural movements made playing easy. Critics said the games

were too simple. After a few years, interest in motion control games fell.

In 2011, Nintendo released *The Legend of Zelda: Skyward Sword* for the Wii console. This game used motion control to create an immersive game experience. Virtual reality (VR) games also gave motion control gaming a second life. Many VR games require the use of motion controllers.

Players See Through Their Character's Eyes

Interesting visuals make video games exciting. In early video games, graphics were 2D. The images were flat and basic. Players' choices of motions were limited. These games featured a third-person point of view. In third-person games, players watch their character move on the screen.

Improvements in 3D graphics made visual designs more exciting. Players could now choose games with a first-person point of view. In first-person games, players experience the game through the characters' eyes. Players feel like they are inside

Press START button

AN **ID** SOFTWARE PRODUCTI

1992

Year that popular first-person game *Wolfenstein 3D* was released.

- The point of view in a video game can impact a player's experience.
- In third-person games, players watch the character on the screen.
- In first-person games, players see through their character's eyes.
- There are advantages and disadvantages to both points of view.

their character. They can see items in their character's hands.

In 1991, id Software released a game called *Catacomb 3-D*. This was a first-person game. Players enjoyed the shift in point of view. Since then, first-person games have grown in popularity.

Some players find it difficult to control a first-person character. Players can only see what their character sees. Third-person games offer players a wider view of the game. Some gamers prefer third-person games for this reason. In modern video games, third-person point of view has improved. Characters can now move in many directions. Improved graphics make third-person games more exciting than past versions. Nintendo's *The Legend of Zelda: Breath of the Wild* is a popular third-person game.

8

Face and Voice Recognition Add New Dimensions

Biometric technology identifies a person through his or her physical traits. Fingerprints are an example of biometrics. Another example is voice recognition. A computer uses voice recognition to take requests from its user. Biometric technology has many purposes. It is used in mobile phones, police stations, and even video games.

In 2010, Microsoft released Kinect. This was an add-on device to the Xbox 360. The Kinect's camera takes a 3D image of the player's

EMOTION SENSORS

In the past, game creators didn't know players' reactions to games. The company Affectiva changed that. Affectiva creates technology that reads people's emotions. This technology allows games to analyze players' facial expressions. One example is the 2016 version of the game *Nevermind*. When players show fear, the game gets harder. Players must control their emotions to do well in the game.

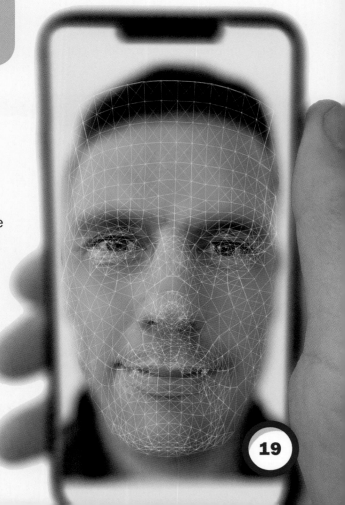

133,333

Kinect units sold per day for the first two months of its release.

- Biometric technology uses people's physical traits to identify them.
- Video games use biometrics to enhance play.
- Players use face and voice recognition to play games on the Xbox with Kinect.

app and their smartphones to scan their faces.

Face recognition will continue to improve over time. The Intel RealSense 3D camera is one example. This advanced camera may allow games to react to players' facial expressions.

body. The system then uses face recognition to identify the player. Some players use face or voice recognition instead of controllers.

In 2011, Sony released the basketball game *NBA 2K15*. Before the start of the game, the console would scan gamers' faces. It then placed the images on characters in the game. This allowed gamers to become characters on the screen. But the scans did not always work well. When *NBA 2K17* came out, its face recognition had improved. Gamers can now use a mobile

Virtual Reality Brings Players Inside the Game

Virtual reality (VR) games use visuals and sound to create a simulation of another world. Players view VR games through a headset. When users put on a VR headset, the virtual world appears before them. The headset allows the user to look up, down, and around. Most headsets display a different image in each eye. This mimics eyes' actions in real life.

The virtual world is similar to a regular video game. But in VR games, the user is inside the game. With the use of a controller, the

user can touch things in the virtual world. Players might find themselves underwater. Or they could be cooking in a kitchen.

Some people experience "simulation sickness" when using VR. This is a type of motion sickness. VR designers are working on ways to stop this motion sickness. To avoid sickness, VR gamers should play for short periods of time.

Stanley Weinbaum was a science fiction writer.

SENSORAMA

In 1962, a filmmaker invented the Sensorama Simulator. The Sensorama had a seat, handles, and viewing holes. When a person sat in the seat, they viewed the 3D movie *Motorcycle*. Vents blew wind on their face. The handles shook like a real motorcycle. Stereo sound delivered the noises of a real engine.

1935
Year that author Stanley G. Weinbaum wrote a story about virtual reality goggles.

- VR is a computer-created environment that feels real to the user.
- VR players use a headset to experience the virtual world.
- The VR user can look up and down and touch things in the virtual world.
- Some people experience motion sickness when playing VR games.

Augmented Reality Combines Real World and Game World

In an augmented reality (AR) game, the real world and the game world combine. AR technology places a computer-created image on a user's view of the real world. Sometimes AR technology adds sound. Most people use mobile devices to play AR games.

Pokémon GO is an AR game. Players download the app on a tablet or smartphone. They then use the app to locate Pokémon characters in their area. When the app is open, the screen shows players their real-world surroundings. AR technology makes Pokémon characters appear on the screen. Players walk around to try to find more Pokémon.

AR IN BOOKS

AR books combine traditional text with digital content. The reader uses a mobile device to access AR books. The AR allows the reader to interact with 3D content. AR books help people learn in new ways.

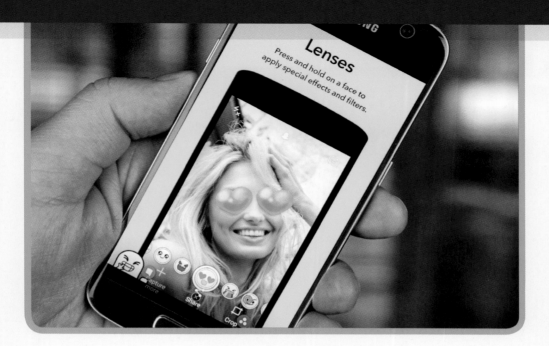

Augmented reality is also used in social media. The app Snapchat has an AR feature called Lenses.

This feature lets users place digital designs over their faces. Popular designs are cat ears or a unicorn horn.

Some companies use AR to increase sales. A furniture store lets shoppers place images of furniture in a digital view of their home. A shoe company lets shoppers digitally "try on" shoes. This allows customers to try out products before buying them. One AR app directs people around cities. Another offers 3D information for museum visitors.

$1.2 billion
Amount that investors gave to AR technology from January to March 2016.

- Augmented reality (AR) combines computer-created images with the real world.
- *Pokémon Go* and Snapchat are both popular AR apps.
- Some companies use AR to help sell their products.

Mobile Gaming Lets People Play Anywhere

Mobile games are played on smartphones, tablets, or other small devices. In 1994, *Tetris* became one of the first mobile games. *Tetris* was a puzzle game first created for the computer. Another early mobile game was *Snake*. It was released by the electronics company Nokia in 1997. These early games were slow and simple. *Snake* appeared as four lines on a green background.

TETRIS

$46.1 billion

Revenue generated by mobile games in 2017.

- Mobile games are played on smartphones, tablets, and other handheld devices.
- In 1994, *Tetris* became one of the first mobile games.
- Mobile gaming became more popular with the invention of the iPhone.
- The App Store allows players to purchase games in an online store.

Wireless application protocol (WAP) came out in 1998. WAP connected mobile devices to the Internet. Now people could download games on their cell phones. They could also play with other people online.

Progress in mobile technology made way for 3D mobile games. In 2007, Apple launched the first iPhone. The iPhone's touch screen allowed players to move more easily. Apple then launched the App Store in 2008. The App Store offered affordable and free mobile games. It helped make iPhones one of the top mobile gaming platforms. Games such as *Fruit Ninja* and *Angry Birds* exploded in popularity. *Candy Crush* was the most downloaded game in 2013.

MMO Games Support Large Numbers of Players

In massively multiplayer online (MMO) games, many gamers play online at the same time. MMOs got their start in offline role-playing games. In role-playing games, players pretend to be someone else. One example is the table game *Dungeons and Dragons*. Similar to role-playing games, MMO players choose an avatar. In many games, players can choose to be an animal, human, or human-like figure.

In 2004, Blizzard Entertainment released *World of Warcraft*. It became one of the most popular MMOs. *World of Warcraft* has a detailed 3D background. It is also played in real time. In real-time games, players do not take turns. Instead, they play at the same time. Players' actions affect other players as the game is going.

World of Warcraft is an MMO that is also a role-playing game. Not all MMOs are role-playing games. However, all MMOs allow players to talk with one another. Gamers meet at a central game location to discuss plans. They then branch out to other areas of the game world.

Many MMOs are cooperative. Players work together to achieve a goal. Throughout the game, players collect and trade items. Other MMOs are competitive. In these games, players win by beating one another.

10 million
Number of people who played *World of Warcraft* in October 2012.

- MMO stands for massively multiplayer online game.
- MMOs can be played online by many players at the same time.
- Many, but not all, MMOs are role-playing games.
- MMOs can be cooperative or competitive.

Fact Sheet

- *Pac-Man* was a wildly popular video arcade game. It came out in 1980 and sold 350,000 game cabinets for arcades. Two years later, *Ms. Pac-Man* was released. It became the best-selling arcade video game of all time.

- *Tetris* was a PC game created by a Russian mathematician in 1984. In 1988, Nintendo added *Tetris* to every Game Boy. The game helped make Game Boy a top-selling handheld console.

- Before home gaming consoles, people went to arcades to play games for a fee. Skee-Ball was the original arcade game. It came out in 1909. In Skee-Ball, players roll balls up an inclined lane. The balls drop into holes at the top of the lane, earning players points.

- Graphics for video games greatly improved after 1990. Designers tried to keep up with breakthroughs in film and television. This led to the use of CGI.

- Before the rise of the internet, the Learning Company released educational games on CD-ROMs. The first educational materials were called Reader Rabbit. These paved the way for many more educational computer games on CD-ROM.

- *Minecraft* is a brick-building game created by a Swedish designer. It came out of the indie game movement in 2010. The indie game movement refers to independent game creators. Improved technology allows game creators to create quality games in small studios.

Glossary

arcade
A public indoor area where people play coin-operated video games.

avatar
A figure that represents a person in a video game.

immersive
The feeling of being completely inside an experience or environment.

operating system
A computer program that controls the computer's basic functions.

processor
The part of a computer that reads most of the computer's data.

resolution
A device's ability to show clear, high-detail images.

scrolling
Moving computer text or images across a screen.

simulation
Something that is meant to look and feel like something else.

two-dimensional
An image with length and width but no depth.

wireless
A computer technology that uses radio waves to transmit data.

For More Information

Books

Hansen, Dustin. *Game On!: Video Game History from Pong and Pac-Man to Mario, Minecraft, and More*. New York: Feiwel & Friends, 2016.

Paris, David, and Stephanie Herweck Paris. *History of Video Games*. Huntington Beach, CA: Teacher Created Materials, 2017.

Ceceri, Kathy. *Video Games: Design and Code Your Own Adventure*. White River Junction, VT: Nomad Press, 2015.

Visit 12StoryLibrary.com

Scan the code or use your school's login at **12StoryLibrary.com** for recent updates about this topic and a full digital version of this book. Enjoy free access to:

- Digital ebook
- Breaking news updates
- Live content feeds
- Videos, interactive maps, and graphics
- Additional web resources

Note to educators: Visit 12StoryLibrary.com/register to sign up for free premium website access. Enjoy live content plus a full digital version of every 12-Story Library book you own for every student at your school.

Index

About the Author

Jamie Kallio is a youth services librarian in the south suburbs of Chicago. She has written many nonfiction books for children. She was also a master at Atari's *Space Invaders.*